FALSE PAPERS

A Story From World War One

SURVIVORS

FALSE PAPERS

A Story From World War One

Stewart Ross

HODDER
Wayland

an imprint of Hodder Children's Books

Book editor: Katie Orchard
Map illustrator: Peter Bull

Published in Great Britain in 2002 by Hodder Wayland
An imprint of Hodder Children's Books Limited

British Library Cataloguing in Publication Data

Ross, Stewart
False Papers: A Story From World War I – (Survivors)
1. World War, 1914–1918 – Juvenile fiction 2. Children's stories
I. Title
823.9'14 [J]

ISBN 0 7502 3873 9

Typeset by Avon Dataset Ltd, Bidford-on-Avon, Warks
www.avondataset.com

Printed and bound in Great Britain by
Clays Ltd, St Ives plc

Introduction

False Papers is based on a story told to me by a family I met while on holiday in France many years ago. I have changed the names of the characters and the village where they lived. Otherwise, the story is largely as I remember it.

From the late seventeenth century onwards, France dominated continental Europe. Its power reached a climax at the time of the Revolution and the Emperor Napoleon (1789–1815). For almost two decades, triumphant French armies spread the revolutionary principles of liberty, equality and fraternity across the continent. It was France's finest hour.

Over the next sixty-five years, France's position was eroded by the growing economic and military power of the states of Germany, headed by Prussia. Matters came to a head in 1870–71, when France suffered a swift embarrassing defeat at the hands of the Prussian army. By the terms of the Treaty of Frankfurt, France was obliged to give up the rich provinces of Alsace and Lorraine to the new German Empire and pay reparations, or compensation, of

5 billion francs (about US$1 billion).

France had rarely experienced such humiliation and thirsted for revenge. In 1914, armed and in league with Britain and Russia, this opportunity finally came.

The opening scenes of *False Papers* are set in a small village in the Vendée, a rural department, or region, in south-west France, in the spring of 1914.

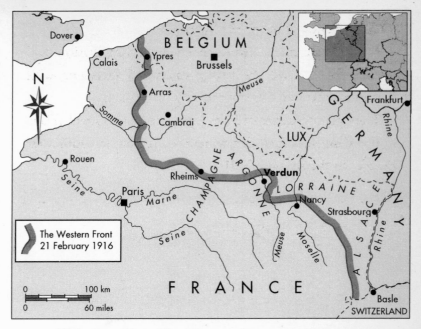

This map shows the Western Front on 21 February 1916, when the 20th Infantry was called to help defend Verdun.

This book is gratefully dedicated to the staff and pupils of Port Regis School, Dorset.

One

Footsteps

I leaned against the side door of the bakery and smiled. At last, after a month of trying, I'd managed to get to work before Sergeant Delarge. Now I could ask Papa for my own key.

He couldn't refuse, could he? Not if I explained to him how I had been kept waiting, forced to hang around in the dark and the cold at three o'clock in the morning.

This wasn't quite true, of course. The church clock had not yet struck three, the time I was supposed to light the bakery fires. The night wasn't cold, either. But the details weren't important. What mattered was that I had proved myself keener than the super-efficient Delarge. For that, I told myself, I deserved to be trusted with my own key, a symbol that I was now an adult.

Like so many young men, I couldn't wait to enter the grown-up world.

Hearing footsteps running along the main street, I moved away from the door and listened. Someone was hurrying in my direction with quick, purposeful strides. Who could it be? Certainly not Delarge, Papa's right-hand man, the heroic veteran of the war in Morocco. Delarge had been so badly wounded in his right leg that he walked with a pronounced limp. No one had ever seen him run.

Keeping close to the bakery wall, I made my way cautiously up the lane towards the main street. The echoing footsteps slowed as they approached. About twenty metres from the bakery, they stopped altogether.

Was it a thief hurrying away from the scene of his crime? I edged further towards the end of the lane, eager to see who it was. The footsteps started again. They were slow and uneven now, a firm tread followed by a pause then a lighter tread. I flattened myself against the rough stones of the wall and waited.

Seconds later, Sergeant Delarge limped round the corner. There were no streetlights in St Frévisse in those days and the lane was as black as a gun barrel. I held my breath as Delarge passed. He paused before the bakery door and let out what sounded like a sigh of relief. The key clicked in the lock, the door swung open and shortly afterwards a pool of yellow light showed that he had lit an oil lamp and started work.

I waited a couple of minutes then entered the bakery as the clock began to strike.

'Good morning, Sergeant Delarge!' I called blearily, trying to sound as if I had just dragged myself out of bed.

'Ah! Monsieur Pierre, good morning!' replied Delarge, who was standing at the far end of the room counting the sacks of flour that the miller had delivered the previous afternoon. 'Three o'clock on the dot! What a punctual young man you are! You'll be here before me one day, won't you? I'll have to be careful.'

I said nothing. Looking across at Delarge I noticed that his forehead was glistening with sweat, as if he had been running.

Tucked away in the south-west, our small community of farmers and craftsmen had only once played an important part in France's history. At the time of the Revolution we had fought like demons to protect our church and our king from the bloodthirsty Parisian revolutionaries and it had taken whole armies to subdue us. But in 1914, almost a century later, these momentous events were just a memory.

It was this, perhaps, that had made Sergeant Delarge something of a hero when he joined us – he reminded us of our past glories and made us proud of France's new empire. No one was sure where he had come from. He just turned up in Bonneau's café one autumn afternoon in 1907, dressed in the threadbare uniform of the 7th African Division, and by eight o'clock that evening he had captivated the hearts of the entire village. His stories of battles with the Arabs and how he had received the wound that had left him an invalid for life held his audience spellbound.

'If it wasn't for that damned scimitar,' he had exclaimed, slapping his injured leg, 'I'd still be at the front!' He rose unsteadily to his feet and saluted. '*Vive la France!*' he cried, draining his glass of anisette.

It wasn't just the men whom the sergeant had won over, either. Although he wasn't handsome – his small, close-set eyes and pointed nose made him look rather like a weasel – he was as popular with the village women as he was with their menfolk. The few who weren't charmed by his flattering city manners were overcome by a desire to mother this poor, lame hero.

Now you know something about Delarge, perhaps you can understand my confusion that dark spring morning. If he had lied about his war wound, then what else was untrue? His battles? His rank? Perhaps even his name?

In my eagerness to become an adult, I had stumbled into falsehood and deceit. Looking back, I realize I should have learned from the experience. But I didn't – and I paid my price.

Two

Hatred

By the time my father came into the shop at seven o'clock that morning I was utterly depressed. I had gone about my work as usual – lighting the fires, mixing and kneading the dough, feeding the loaves into the oven on long-handled shovels – but my mind was in turmoil.

At first, I thought I might have been mistaken about Delarge. Perhaps someone else had run down the street, seen him and fled? The noise of running footsteps would have covered the sergeant's halting approach. But, no. If that had happened, Delarge would have said something. Besides, it didn't explain the sweat on his forehead.

After going through the matter a thousand times, I realized there was only one possible answer. Delarge had been running. In which case, he did not have an injured leg; or, if he did, the injury was a lot less serious than he made out. In either case, the man was a fraud.

The conclusion was no comfort. I had no proof.

It would be the word of Pierre Clouet, a fourteen-year-old baker's son, against that of Sergeant Delarge of the 7th African Division, a respected war veteran. It didn't take a genius to work out who would be believed.

What could I do? Even my plan of asking Papa for a key to the bakery was in ruins. If I admitted that I had arrived before the trusted Delarge, my father would be bound to mention it to him. Delarge's suspicions would then be aroused and he might turn nasty to stop me blowing his cover.

There was nothing I *could* do. For the time being, I just had to wait and watch.

Delarge and I used to take it in turns to help Papa in the front of the shop while the other worked in the bakery behind. Today it was my turn at the counter.

I did my best to appear normal, greeting each customer with a smile, as Papa had taught me, and listening politely to their village gossip. As St Frévisse was only a small village, we knew everyone by name and usually had their orders ready before they asked for them: two loaves for Père Gérard, a small one for Mademoiselle Gislain, six for Alouette, the maid from the big house by the crossroads, and so on.

The talk, as it had been for the last year, was a mixture of local gossip and the growing threat of war with Germany.

'. . . And Madame Bertrand saw her out last night, past ten it was and quite dark . . .'

'. . . Three divisions, all marching up and down near the border . . .'

'. . . And he told her his brother said we'll be in Berlin within a fortnight, before the Germans have even had time to pull on their boots . . .'

'. . . So they said they'd go on strike if they didn't get more . . .'

Around mid-morning, Mama called in to collect our bread. She always looked so young and cheerful that the whole shop brightened up when she entered. She was Papa's second wife, fifteen years younger than him. His first wife, Hélène, had died in childbirth in 1890, leaving him with two daughters, Thèrese and Virginie. My half-sisters were both now married with children of their own.

Papa's second marriage, nine years after Hélène's death, was a great surprise to everyone. As he never tired of telling us, he had watched my mother growing up until, one day, he suddenly realized he was in love with her and pursued her relentlessly until she agreed to accompany him to the altar.

'She was, still is and always will be the prettiest *petit four* in the land,' he used to declare proudly.

I was the only child of their marriage, born exactly two

years after their wedding day. When I was younger, Papa referred to me affectionately as his 'little croissant'. It was assumed that one day the sign above the shop would read: *Joseph Clouet & Son, Bakers*.

Perhaps it was because of what I had learned earlier that morning, but for some reason, as I watched my parents chatting, a sense of uneasiness came over me. Today Mama seemed distracted. She nodded mechanically in answer to my father's questions and every now and again glanced towards the door to the bakehouse. It was as if she was expecting – even hoping – to see someone there.

Mama stayed in the shop longer than usual. When Madame Gilbert and several other women came in, Mama moved aside and lingered by the cake display.

Madame Gilbert asked for a loaf from the shelf beside the bakehouse door. As I turned to get it, the door opened and Delarge appeared. Ignoring me completely, he glanced around the shop, recognized someone and smiled.

I turned to see who he was looking at. As I did so, Mama blushed and walked out of the front door without a word.

From that moment onwards I hated Delarge.

Three

Confrontation

Delarge was a clever man. Although I attempted to hide my feelings towards him, he soon sensed that something was wrong and tried, with subtle hints and questions, to find out what it was.

We were like two boxers edging cautiously round each other, watching and waiting for the other to drop his guard. Delarge sought to open me up with jabs and feints. I backed off, acting innocent and refusing to let him see the anger that boiled within me. In the end, though, I could contain myself no longer.

It was early one Monday morning and we were resting after putting the first batch of loaves into the oven. The previous day, as every Sunday, Delarge had come to our house for lunch. Afterwards, he had suggested we all go for a walk. Papa declined, saying he was tired and wanted a nap. I'd made an excuse about wanting to read and Mama and Delarge had gone out on their own.

Leaning against the dough vat, I watched Delarge taking a drink of water. I recalled the smug look on his face when he had returned from the walk with Mama. How I detested him! Everything about him – his thin hands, his fat lips and his tiny animal eyes – revolted me.

Delarge put down his mug and glanced across at me. 'Enjoy your book, Monsieur Pierre?' he asked.

It was a moment before I realized what he was talking about. When I understood, I thought he had been reading my mind. 'OK, Monsieur Delarge,' I muttered. I always called him 'Monsieur' now, instead of 'Sergeant', although he had not remarked upon it. 'Better than walking, anyway.'

'Really? I always find a walk after a meal helps the digestion. You should try it.'

My patience finally snapped. 'I didn't want to spoil your walk, Monsieur Delarge!' I blurted out. 'Besides, I thought you didn't like walking because of your terrible injury?' I spat out the last two words with all the sarcasm I could muster.

The moment I had finished, I knew I had made a mistake. Delarge had obviously suspected I knew something was going on between him and my mother. But until that moment I don't think he realized that I also knew about his leg.

Very slowly, moving with an exaggerated limp, he crossed the floor towards me. My heart was thumping like a cannon. I thought he was going to hit me and I tensed my muscles for a fight.

When there was no more than a few centimetres between us, he stopped. I was tall for my age, about the same height as Delarge, and strong, too. If it had come to a fight, I think I could have matched him. But he did not strike. Instead, he stood quite still and fixed me with his dark, narrow eyes, like a snake.

Standing so close that I felt his breath on my face, he said coldly, 'Listen carefully, Monsieur Pierre. Maybe you know something, maybe you don't. But you understand nothing. Nothing at all. You are a boy, not a man. Take my advice and don't meddle in the adult world, OK? I wouldn't want you to get hurt . . .'

He took a step backwards and clasped his hands before his chest as if in prayer. 'Believe me, Monsieur Pierre,' he went on, 'there will soon be many changes. You will not be able to stop them. No one will. When France goes to war, all able-bodied men will be called up. Then only you and me and the old gaffers will be left. So let's be friends, eh?'

He extended his hand toward me but I did not take it. I couldn't move. My mind was reeling at what he had said. He seemed to have threatened me and at the same time taken me into his confidence. Was his plan to wait for war and then take over when Papa had gone? I couldn't believe it!

I needed fresh air. Without saying a word, I turned and ran out of the darkened bakery into the early morning sunlight.

Once in the street, I began running towards home. I hadn't gone far when I met Papa on his way to the bakery. 'What's the matter, Pierre?' he asked anxiously. 'You look as if you've seen a ghost.'

'I'm not well, Papa,' I panted, trying not to meet his eyes. 'I need to see Mama.'

'All right. Sergeant Delarge and I can manage. You take it easy – although I'm sure running won't make you feel any better.'

His kindness was almost more than I could bear. After a few steps, I stopped and called back to him.

'Yes, Pierre?'

'I think I ought to tell you . . .' Seeing the worried look in his eyes, I hesitated. I couldn't go on. 'It's nothing, Papa. I'll be OK.'

I found Mama alone in the scullery, sorting through the washing. 'Mama!' I cried, shutting the door and leaning against it to get my breath back. 'I need to talk to you!'

Four

The Storm Breaks

I can still picture my mother as she was then. Standing beside the linen table with the sunshine streaming through the scullery window behind her, she looked like a saint in stained glass.

'Pierre, darling, what on earth's the matter?' she asked.

Above her pale blue dress with its high collar of white lace, my mother's oval face and bright green eyes looked so beautiful. Even before I spoke, I knew I wouldn't be able to tell her.

'I'm worried, Mama.'

'What about? Are you working too hard? Is it all the talk of war?'

The question gave me a way out. 'Yes, war. If war breaks out, will you be all right? I'm frightened.'

She led me to a chair. 'Sit down, Pierre,' she said calmly, sitting next to me and putting her hand on my arm. 'Now listen to me. If there is a war – and it's a big "if" – then it will take place in the east, hundreds of kilometres from here. There won't be any fighting in the Vendée.'

'But conscription – what if Papa is called up?'

She laughed. 'Your father is forty-five, my love. He won't be going anywhere.'

'But Monsieur Delarge said . . .' Did I feel her hand stiffen slightly or was it my imagination?

'Yes? What did he say?'

Again, I didn't say what I wanted to. 'He said *all* men, apart from the old gaffers, would have to go.'

Mama turned her face towards me. When she spoke, her voice was low and thoughtful, as if she had just realized something. 'Did he? Well he's jumping the gun a bit, Pierre. You don't want to believe everything you hear, even from Sergeant Delarge.'

Relief swept over me. 'You mean he's not always right?'

'Not always. I think he sometimes gets a bit carried away. Probably the result of his army experiences – they were terrible, you know, poor man.'

'Were they?' I asked sarcastically.

'What do you mean? Of course they were! You've seen how he can hardly walk.'

'I can't miss that! After all, I work with him all day.'

Mama laughed. 'Pierre! I am beginning to think there's a streak of unkindness in you . . .' She stood up and pulled me to my feet beside her. 'Come on, young man, no more of this time wasting! I've got the laundry to sort out and your father and Sergeant Delarge will be rushed off their feet without you.'

As I was leaving, she said, 'Remember, Pierre, you having nothing to worry about.'

I paused with my hand on the scullery door. 'Nothing?'

'Nothing in the whole wide world. I promise.'

I wonder, if she had known what I knew, whether she would have promised quite so readily.

Spring eased into summer. By June the bakery was so hot, even in the small hours of the morning, that Delarge and I worked stripped to the waist. When his back was turned, I looked over his body for scars of old wounds. I was not surprised to find his skin unblemished and the muscles beneath it scrawny and weak, quite unlike a soldier's.

Despite my continued misgivings, however, we got on well enough. I found it easier to be civil to Delarge because whatever had happened – real or imagined – between my mother and him seemed to have ended. There were no more blushes or knowing glances or walks together in the countryside. At least, not then.

On Sunday afternoons I used to meet with David and Ghislain, two of my old classmates who now worked as farmhands. We messed about by the river, throwing stones and talking carelessly about local girls and the possibility of war. I sometimes considered sharing my knowledge about Delarge with them, but never did so. They wouldn't have believed me. Even if they had, I couldn't have trusted them to keep the secret. And if it leaked out, we would have been in serious trouble for mocking a hero of France.

The only other person I thought about sharing my secret with was Aurelie Blanche, the eldest daughter of our widowed postmaster. We had known each other all our lives and I think our parents secretly hoped we would marry one day. Such arrangements were quite common in small, old-fashioned village communities like ours.

Aurelie was a practical girl and quite attractive, too, with a broad mouth and a small, freckled nose. Our relationship wasn't romantic but we enjoyed chatting when we chanced to meet. In the end I decided that, of all my friends, she alone would give me a fair hearing. So, when she came into the shop on Sunday 2 August, I slipped her a note without my father seeing. It asked her to meet me on the bridge at 2 pm the following Sunday.

That meeting never took place. From late June the clouds hovering on the horizon had begun to thicken alarmingly. Within a month they lowered over the entire land. Finally, on 3 August, the storm broke.

France went to war.

Five

Visitors

The past is a landscape that changes with the light. On a bright summer's day, it is clear and full of joy; beneath the grey skies of autumn, the same scene is a dreary vista of bleakness and despair.

So it was with the day that France went to war.

The announcement came through from Paris on Monsieur Blanche's telegraph. Hatless, he rushed into the street waving his arms and yelling, 'War! War at last! It's come! *Vive la France!*'

As the news spread around the commune, we abandoned our counters, workshops and fields and gathered in the main street for an evening of wild celebration. At last we had a chance to get our revenge for the humiliation of 1870–71.

For a few sweet weeks we remembered the party as one of the happiest days of our lives. But then, as the cruel reality of the slaughter seeped into the village like a plague, the light began to change. Now we look back with infinite sadness on the dancing, singing and endless toasts to victory drunk in our rough local wine. It was not, as we had believed, a party that heralded victory, but a frenzied wake for a lost generation.

All young Frenchmen had to do military service. Before the war, the well-off and well educated, like the Pétaud boys from the old Puy-Greffier castle, managed to get away with doing very little.

That all changed in wartime. Rich and poor, learned and illiterate, every able-bodied young man flocked to sign up. It was not just duty – it was an honour and an opportunity. Everyone wanted to smash the Germans as they had smashed us over forty years before.

The recruits gathered at dawn on Wednesday morning. The whole village came to see them off. I caught sight of Aurelie standing by the lime trees and made my way over to her.

'It's exciting, isn't it?' she cried, standing on tiptoe to see over the heads of the crowd.

'Very,' I agreed. 'You read my note?'

'Yes. But hang on, Pierre! Look, there's Paul!' She started waving. 'Hello Paul! Don't forget the Dresden China figure you promised me! Good luck!'

I felt miserable and without really thinking said, 'I'm

afraid I can't make Sunday, Aurelie. Something's cropped up.'

Her face fell. 'Oh, Pierre! I was really looking forward to it.'

'Sorry. Maybe another time.' I turned away and went to join my mother and father in front of the bakery.

A few minutes later, the band struck up and the column of men began to move. 'To Berlin!' they cried, waving and blowing kisses to the girls. 'Berlin or death!'

As I watched them march past the church and out into the countryside beyond, a wave of envy came over me. I wanted to be with them. I longed to be a soldier, to pull on the noble uniform, shoulder my own rifle and fight like a tiger for the country I loved.

It was then, with the farewell shouts of the recruits still ringing in my ears, that an idea flickered across my mind. As I've already mentioned, I looked much older than my fourteen years. I was sure, therefore, if I could get hold of false identity papers, I'd be able to enlist.

But where could I find the necessary documents?

My brothers-in-law, Bruno and Louis, were in that first batch of men to leave the village. Three weeks later, an army staff car drove into the village and parked in front of the church. I was serving in the bakery on my own at the time and, watching through the window, I saw two men in uniform get out and look around. Shortly afterwards, Madame Gilbert shuffled into view. The soldiers called her over to them, saluted and started talking to her.

Fascinated, I saw Madame Gilbert nod several times then point in the direction of the bakery. The soldiers saluted once more, did a sharp left turn and marched straight towards our shop.

'Good morning, young man!' said the taller of the two soldiers as he entered. He was a captain, a broad-shouldered man with a large, bushy moustache. 'You work here regularly?'

My heart jumped. I couldn't believe it – was he really going to ask me to join up?

'Yes, sir,' I replied in what I hoped sounded like a military manner. 'But it's rather boring. I'd much rather be in the arm—'

'Hang on, son!' interrupted the captain with a smile. 'Your turn will come. Just wait a year or two, till you're old enough.'

I was encouraged and deflated by the remark. The man obviously thought I looked older than I was. But even a year or two was too long – our soldiers would be celebrating their victory in the cafés of Berlin long before that.

'No, it's not you we're after,' the captain went on. 'We

want to speak with a Sergeant Delarge. He works here, doesn't he?'

Delarge! Were they on to him at last?

'Yes, sir!' I said eagerly. 'I'll get him for you right away.'

Six

The Volunteer

I opened the door to the bakehouse and called out loudly, 'Monsieur Delarge! Could you come into the shop please? Some gentlemen want to talk to you.'

I had to hand it to Delarge. Even if he had never served as a soldier, he certainly gave a good impression of having done so. The moment he set eyes on the captain, he stiffened and raised his arm in a salute. 'Sergeant Delarge, honourably discharged from the 7th African Division, at your service, sir!' he barked.

The visitors seemed somewhat taken aback by this military display. 'Thank you, Sergeant,' said the captain, casually returning the salute. 'We'd like you to undertake a small task for us.'

The corners of Delarge's fleshy mouth rose in a slight smile at the officer's request. 'Anything you say, sir!' he replied eagerly.

The officer raised an eyebrow. 'Of course, Sergeant. As

you know, we need all the men we can get. St Frévisse and the other villages around here have already provided a good number of recruits. First class, some of them.'

'Glad to hear it, sir!' said Delarge.

The officer gave him an irritated glance, then continued, 'Even so, we need more. We're setting up village recruitment committees of respected citizens – chaps like yourself, old soldiers and so on – to do a spot of recruiting for us. You know the kind of men we're after: shirkers who pretend to be sick, men who are technically past the recruiting age but are perfectly fit to fight, that sort of thing.'

I looked at Delarge. There was a gleam in his eye that had not been there before.

'So, if you'd agree to look after the St Frévisse Recruitment Committee,' the officer went on, 'we'll go down to the café, have a drink and sort out the paperwork. What do you say, Sergeant?'

'I'm your man, sir. Only too pleased to be of assistance. I'm sure we'll be able to round up a few skivers. We've got a few fit oldies, too. Dying to do their bit, some of them.'

Once Delarge was installed as chairman of our recruitment committee, it was only a matter of time before Papa joined up. What else could he do? He was above the normal age for army service, of course, but his health was good. His sons-in-law had gone off to fight, he explained, so why shouldn't he? Besides, as a leading member of the community, the employer of the Recruitment Committee Chairman, he had to set an example.

The fateful decision was taken one Sunday lunchtime in September. By the time dessert was served, my parents had grown quite heated over the issue. Papa was arguing his case for joining up while Mama passionately begged him not to. Delarge was present, as always, but he kept strangely quiet. His only contribution was in answer to a plea from my mother.

'Sergeant Delarge,' she had asked, 'I beg you, explain to my husband that France will win the war without him. Tell him he's not needed!'

Delarge smiled. 'My dear Madame Clouet,' he began, 'far be it from me to intervene in family matters. They are none of my business. Nevertheless, since you press me, allow me to set out the position as I see it. 'As Chairman of the St Frévisse Recruitment Committee, I should mention that men older and less fit than your husband have been signed up. Furthermore, it is becoming clear that victory will not be as easy or as swift as we had hoped. Even now, Paris, our great capital, is in danger.' He turned to my father. 'On the other hand, speaking as your grateful employee, sir, the last thing I want is for you to leave. I would lose my job, the village would be without a baker—'

'*Rubbish!*' interrupted my father. 'You could run the bakery, Delarge.'

Delarge raised his hands in surprise. 'Me, sir?'

'Come off it, man!' muttered Papa. 'If you can lead a platoon into battle, you can certainly run a village bakery!'

'That's not the point, Joseph!' exclaimed Mama. 'I don't want you to go! I need you here. Pierre needs you. Do we mean nothing to you?'

Papa laid his hands on the table and leaned towards her. 'My dearest Marie, please don't torture me. You know I love you more than anything in the world. There is nothing I wouldn't do for you and Pierre. That is why I must join the army. To protect those whom I love.'

Mama's lips were trembling and her pretty face was stained with tears. 'You're going then, Joseph?' she whispered.

'I am, my dear. May God protect us all!'

With a terrible cry of anguish, Mama rose from the table. 'No, Joseph!' she howled. 'God cannot help us! It's too late!' Still sobbing, she left the room and ran upstairs.

When she had gone, Delarge slowly raised his glass and drank – as if he were making a silent toast to the future.

Seven

Depression

Papa left at 8 am on Tuesday 8 October. Captain Brissot, the soldier who had come to the bakery looking for Delarge, drove him away in his car. There were no marching bands or waving girls, just Mama and I standing together in a cold autumn drizzle. It was a pathetic farewell, more like seeing a prisoner off to jail than a soldier to the front.

When the car had disappeared from sight, Mama said calmly, 'Come in now, Pierre. There's nothing to see. He's gone.'

Inside the house, I expected Mama to weep or at least talk to me for a while. She did neither. After clearing away the breakfast things in silence, she went up to her room and remained there until I went to work.

Mama had been like this from the moment Papa had decided to join up. There were no more hysterical outbursts and, as far as I knew, she didn't try to persuade him to change his mind. She was like a wooden puppet, drained of emotion. Even when she bade Papa farewell, she did no more than put her lips to his cheek as if he were leaving for the bakery. The pained look in his eyes told me how much this hurt him. But he didn't say anything. I suppose he didn't want to leave with an argument.

As planned, Delarge was now in charge of the bakery. Instead of being pompous and bullying, as I had feared, he treated me and my twelve-year-old cousin, André, who came to work in the shop, with sickening respect. He insisted on referring to me as his 'young master'. If he wanted me to unload the flour or take a turn behind the counter, he would twist his hands and whine, 'If you have time, Monsieur Clouet, would you mind . . . ?' or, 'It would be so helpful, Monsieur Clouet, if you would . . .'

I reckoned this revolting behaviour was part of Delarge's diabolical master plan: get Papa out of the way, win me over, and move in on Mama. Although he had succeeded with phase one, I resolved that he would get no further. I still called him 'Monsieur Delarge' and limited my conversations with him strictly to matters of business.

In early November Delarge tried a new tactic. When we were alone in the shop together one morning, he said suddenly, 'I think, Monsieur Clouet, that it's time you received proper wages for your work. The allowance your

27

father paid you is no longer appropriate for someone in your position.'

For a few seconds I was tempted by the offer. But I refused, saying coldly, 'Thank you, Monsieur Delarge, but I'd rather not take Papa's money while he's away.'

'Of course, Monsieur Clouet!' Delarge replied, hiding his disappointment with a sour smile. 'How foolish of me to suggest the idea! Please forget I mentioned it.'

I did not forget and mentioned it to Mama that evening. 'Really?' she replied, glancing up from her sewing. 'I suppose you were right, Pierre. Nothing of your father's must be touched.' Her voice was flat and lifeless, as if she were reciting something she had learned by heart.

Mama hardly went out of the house now. She didn't attend Mass or visit friends. She lost interest in her appearance, too, and forgot to ask the cook to prepare meals. Alouette, the girl who helped with the housework, got away with doing almost nothing.

By the end of November, Mama's depression had seeped through the house like an evil odour. My attempts at conversation with her, even on the most routine matters, were fruitless and I no longer looked forward to coming home after work. It was like sharing the house with a stranger or, worse still, a living corpse.

To my relief, Delarge made no mention of the change.

Warned by some animal instinct, he kept his distance. He no longer had Sunday lunch with us and spoke to Mama only on the rare occasions when she came into the shop. He was in no hurry.

In my loneliness, I renewed my friendship with Aurelie. We met in secret on Sunday afternoons and walked for hours through the dying countryside. She was a sympathetic listener and full of wise advice. When I told her about Mama, Aurelie said the condition was probably due to the great strain my mother was under and suggested I should write and tell my father of my worries.

Taking Aurelie's advice, I mentioned my anxiety in the next letter I wrote to my father. I was not surprised when he made no mention of it. The tone of his letters had changed over the weeks he had been away. He didn't talk about home any more, or even what he was doing. Instead, he filled page after page with what seemed like trivial matters. One letter described in minute detail the profusion of wild flowers growing on the battlefield.

I believed he was holding something back from us – something he couldn't or didn't want to mention.

Eight

Murder!

Sixty-three men from St Frévisse went to war in 1914. The majority were front-line troops, so it was surprising we had no casualties until early December. On 3 December we heard that a peasant farmer with land near the Braslet woods had been shot in the stomach. The next day we learned that one of our neighbours had had his right arm blown off.

By Christmas the injury list had risen to seven.

Bruno, husband of my half-sister, Thérèse, and father of her five children, was St Frévisse's first fatality.

Thérèse received the letter from the Ministry of War on 31 December. Two days later, haggard and hollow-eyed behind her veil, she brought the document into the shop to show me. Infantryman Bruno Paullet, I read, had been killed fighting bravely for the glory of France. There were no further details.

Unsure what to say, I muttered, 'He was a very brave man, Thérèse.'

'One of the best, Pierre,' she said firmly. 'He gave up his life, like Jesus Christ, to save us all. He was a hero, a real hero.'

Thèrese's words raised a flood of emotions in me. Pity and admiration mingled with shame: Bruno was a hero – my other brother-in-law, Louis, was a hero – my own father was a hero – but I, Pierre Clouet, was nothing but a simple baker's boy. It was hateful!

Delarge, André and I wore black ties and armbands as a mark of respect for Bruno and his widow. At my suggestion, Delarge agreed to provide Thèrese with all the bread she wanted, free of charge.

When Mama heard that Bruno had been killed, she said simply, as if she had been expecting the news, 'Ah! It has begun!'

Louis was killed a month later. This time the Ministry gave more details of what had happened: he had been shot, they said, defending a position near the River Marne.

Louis' death upset me more than Bruno's had done. Virginie, his widow, had always been my favourite half-sister and I felt her sorrow keenly. Equally distressing was the information the Ministry had provided about where Louis had died.

No one knew precisely where the men were. The names of towns and other features were censored from their letters in case they revealed military secrets. I had been quite surprised, therefore, by a remark Papa had made in a letter that had reached us in mid-January. It was bitterly cold, he had written, so cold that there was ice on the Marne.

The next morning, as we were unloading the ovens, I said casually to André, 'Louis was killed near the Marne.'

'Really? Where's that?' André replied. Geography had been his worst subject at school.

'It's to the east of Paris,' I explained. 'Near where a lot of the fighting is. Papa's there, too.'

André stopped what he was doing and looked up at me, his eyes bright with excitement. 'You mean he's in the thick of it?' he asked. 'Bet you wish you were with him!'

'Not half!' I replied. I meant what I said. It was not just that I wanted to be in the army. I also felt, for Mama's sake as much as anything else, that my middle-aged father needed protecting.

'Do you think he's OK?' I continued.

André laughed. 'Of course he's OK, Pierre! Sergeant Delarge said there's going to be massive new attack in the spring. We're going to smash the Boche and kill thousands of them and march all the way to Berlin—'

'Delarge said that?' I interrupted.

'Yes. He's been a soldier, hasn't he? He knows everything that's going on!'

'Of course!' I said. 'Delarge knows everything.' I returned to my work, wishing I'd never started the conversation.

On Wednesday 3 March 1915 — a date I will never forget — Mama made one of her rare appearances in the shop. She was more animated than she had been for weeks.

After collecting her bread, to my surprise and delight she stayed chatting with me for several minutes. Her eyes were bright, almost fiery, and several times she leaned across the counter to kiss me.

As I was wondering what had caused the happy transformation, she suddenly reached down into her basket and took out a piece of paper.

'Oh, I almost forgot, Pierre! I received this letter this morning. Read it!'

I felt sick the moment I saw the black lettering on the envelope. It was from the Ministry of War. My hands shook uncontrollably as I drew out the familiar-looking letter. One glance was enough.

My lips quivered. Tears blurred my vision. 'Papa!' I cried. 'Oh, no! Not Papa!'

Through my sobs, I became aware of another sound. Looking up, I saw Mama standing before the cake rack. She was pounding hysterically at the delicacies with her fists. Red jam smeared her hands and the front of her blue dress. She was screaming over and over again in a thin, high-pitched voice, 'Murder! Murder! Murder!'

Nine

The Stranger

Sudden death is easier to bear in wartime than in peace. It is less unexpected. There is some consolation, too, in sharing the sorrow of bereavement with others. Nevertheless, it is the most devastating of human experiences.

For a time, I was haunted by the realization that I would never see my father again. Realities had become memories: my father raising his hat and bidding good day to everyone he passed in the street; his loud, open laugh; the homely aroma of tobacco as he enjoyed an after-dinner smoke; and, most poignant of all, the reassuring clasp of his arm round my shoulders as we walked home together from work.

The village was kind and supportive. Before 1916, three deaths in the same family was regarded as extreme misfortune, and people went out of their way to help us. Their generosity meant that my half-sisters never lacked clothes for their children. Several well-off families, such as the Pétauds, increased their daily bread order to help the bakery. Madame Gilbert, who couldn't stand cakes, ordered a fresh one each week.

Everyone mentioned how well my mother coped with her bereavement. I had to agree with them. After her fit of hysterics in the shop, a group of women took her home. I joined her not long afterwards and was astonished to find her calm and open, just as she had been before Papa's decision to leave. She welcomed me with her old smile, took me in her arms and comforted me with the kindest words and gestures.

At the time, I believed Mama was making an effort to appear normal for my sake. But when, after a day or two, there was still no sign of her hysteria or depression, I asked how she really felt.

'Aren't you sad, Mama?' I asked, perching on the arm of the chair in which she was sitting.

'Sad? Of course I am, Pierre, darling,' she replied. 'I'm terribly, deeply sad. But I'm not shocked or even surprised.'

'Why not?'

Mother took my hand and began playing with the fingers. 'For some reason, Pierre – I can't explain why – I knew your father was going to die. I sensed it the instant he decided to join up. You remember that Sunday afternoon? I felt we were being controlled by forces outside ourselves.'

'Is that why you were so miserable?' I asked.

'Yes. I'm sorry, Pierre, I really am. I couldn't help it. I suppose I was mourning your father before he died. Do you understand?'

'I think so,' I replied. 'But what about Mr Delarge?'

Mother's grip on my hand tightened. 'What about him, Pierre? You don't like him, do you?'

'No, I don't. I've never told anyone, but I don't believe he's honest. I sometimes think he persuaded Papa to join up.'

'He certainly didn't!' Mama cried. 'What would he want to do that for? So he could run the bakery while Papa was away, is that what you think?'

'Maybe,' I replied, feeling uncomfortable. 'Or something else.'

'Such as?'

'I don't know,' I lied.

Mama gave my hand a squeeze. 'Come on, Pierre! No more brooding! We must look to the future – I'm sure it's what your father would have wanted.'

That night, lying awake and thinking of Papa, I tried looking into the future as Mama had suggested. The vision was blurred and dark.

Now Mama's depression had lifted, I detected an

unpleasant change in Delarge. He whistled at work and greeted customers with flamboyant good humour. I was irritated and felt my old hatred returning with a new intensity. What I disliked most was the way he seemed to mock my father with exaggerated praise. In the end, two days after my sixteenth birthday, I could take no more.

'An example to us all,' I overheard him saying to a customer one afternoon. 'What strength it must have taken to leave a thriving business and a pretty young wife! What a sacrifice!'

'Who are you talking about, Monsieur Delarge?' I cried, entering the shop from the bakery.

'Your father, of course, Monsieur Pierre!' said Delarge, looking startled.

'Then *don't!*' I shouted. 'You disgust me, Delarge! Don't ever mention my father again, understand?'

Without waiting to hear his reply, I stormed from the shop and headed for the open countryside.

My mind was in such a turmoil of fury and frustration that I didn't care where I was going. Half-walking, half-running, I plunged on across fields and streams until it was so dark I couldn't see more than a few steps in front of me and I had to stop. I was on the edge of a wood. Peering into the darkness, I noticed a light shining through the trees and made my way cautiously towards it. The glow came from a fire burning on the far side of a small glade. The dishevelled figure of a man was crouching beside the flames, warming himself.

Deciding he was a tramp who could probably direct me back to the village, I stepped forward into the firelight.

Ten

Comrade

'Hello!' I called, advancing across the glade. 'Can you tell me where I am, please?'

The tramp took one look at me and fled into the trees. I called after him, explaining that I didn't wish him any harm. I simply wanted directions back to St Frévisse.

'Go away!' came a voice out of the darkness. 'Leave me alone! I've got a gun!'

'Well I haven't,' I replied, holding out my empty hands. 'And I can't leave because I don't know where to go. I'm lost.'

'How do I know it's not a trick?' asked the tramp. 'Anyway, what are you doing here?'

In a few sentences I explained how I had left the village after an argument with a so-called sergeant who had mocked my dead father. My words seemed to calm the tramp. Covering me with a rusty military rifle, he advanced out of the shadows.

I was surprised to see that he was a young man, probably still in his late teens. Although his face was unshaven and his clothes were ragged and filthy, I noticed that his boots were quite new. He spoke in an educated manner, too, and had an air of someone who had seen better days. I was intrigued.

'So you don't like this "sergeant"?' the stranger said. 'Well, tell me the full story. If I like it, I might help you. If I don't, I'll shoot you. Do we have a bargain?'

I didn't believe the man's threat. But rather than risk finding out whether he meant it, I proceeded to recount the story of my life over the last year.

When I had finished, the young vagabond lowered his rifle, sat down by the fire and indicated that I join him. As I did so, he took out a bottle and, after taking a long drink, passed it over to me. 'Go on,' he prompted. 'It's not poison.'

I raised the bottle to my lips and drank. I was not used to spirits and the rough liquid made my eyes water.

'Good, eh?' said the tramp. I nodded and handed the bottle back to him.

'Now it's my turn,' he said, taking another drink and placing the bottle carefully on the ground beside him. 'Listen to Jerôme Villequin, comrade. He'll tell you secrets no one else has dared tell you.'

Jerôme was a communist. Before the war he had been a student in Paris. Although he disapproved of the war – he called it a 'capitalist-imperialist conspiracy', whatever that meant – he had been drafted into the army and sent to the front.

There, he said, his worst fears had been confirmed. Beneath the cloak of patriotism swarmed every injustice imaginable: incompetence, snobbery, bullying, arrogance and, worst of all, endless, pointless slaughter. After five months he had deserted. Since then he had been hiding in the countryside, living off food and drink he stole from isolated farms. He was making his way to the coast, he explained, from where he hoped to take a ship to America.

As Jerôme recounted his story, my amazement changed to bewilderment, then fury. The man was nothing but a liar and a coward. How dared he run away and leave my father to die! And yet, as I listened, a plan was forming in my mind. I wouldn't turn in this lily-livered communist, I decided. At least, not until I had got hold of his identification papers.

When Jerôme had finished, I feigned friendship. I wanted to know more about communism, I said enthusiastically, and might be able to help him get to the coast. I told him I would return the following night with money and food.

'And drink,' he added eagerly. 'I must have a drink.'

'Of course!' I replied. 'I won't forget the drink.'

He clasped me to his stinking chest, thanked me and called me a 'true comrade'. Eventually, after several more handshakes, he gave me directions for the Cholet road that led to St Frévisse and I set off into the darkness.

I found the highway without difficulty and, guided by the stars, headed west for St Frévisse. During the two hours it took me to reach the village I went through my plan. But the more I thought about it, the more doubts I had. So many things could go wrong. And there was my duty towards my mother to think about, too. By the time I reached the Trissot's farm on the outskirts of the village, I had decided to abandon my scheme and hand Jerôme over to the authorities in the morning.

To save time, I left the Cholet road some two hundred metres before the church and cut across the fields towards the rear of our house. As I approached, wondering how I was going to explain my absence to Mama, the back door opened. A figure appeared, silhouetted against the light, then disappeared into the shadows.

Although I was still some distance away and had caught only a fleeting glimpse of the visitor, I recognized him immediately.

It was Delarge.

Eleven

Jerôme Villequin

I wanted to confront Delarge there and then. But I was worried about waking the neighbours and so decided to follow him to his home and tackle him there.

Although Delarge had disappeared, I was fairly sure I could find him again. He lived on his own in a small cottage beyond the church. To get there, he'd have to skirt round the back of our street to the Cholet road, go up to the crossroads and then turn left towards the church. I ran back across the fields and, keeping to the edge of the road, began advancing towards the crossroads.

My hunch was right. By the light of the stars I spotted Delarge about thirty metres ahead of me hurrying towards the centre of the village. He was walking normally, with no sign of a limp. I quickened my pace to keep up with him. As I did so, a dog began barking somewhere to my left.

Delarge stopped and looked round. There was nowhere to hide.

'Hello,' he called softly. Adopting his false limp, he began walking back towards me. 'Is that you, Monsieur Clouet?'

'You know it is!' I replied.

My heart was thumping wildly as I advanced to meet him. When we were no more than a metre apart, he halted and said, 'Fancy meeting you, Monsieur Clouet. It's very late. Does your mother know you're out?'

'You tell me, Delarge,' I replied. I made no attempt to disguise my scorn. 'You have just come from our house.'

'From your house, Monsieur Clouet? Really! What gave you that idea?'

His sarcastic manner infuriated me. 'I saw you!' I hissed. 'And I saw you walking normally!' I was rapidly losing control of myself. 'You're a fraud, Delarge! A cheat, a liar, a coward . . .'

I'm not sure who moved first. I think it was Delarge. But I was too quick for him. As he lunged towards me, I stepped aside and hit him as hard as I could on the temple. With a groan, he fell forward into the road, struck his head against a stone, and lay still.

Horrified, I saw a dark stain seep from the corner of Delarge's mouth. Oh, my God! I thought. I've killed him!

I was seized with panic. What could I do? I couldn't go

home. I had to get away. But where? I remembered Jerôme and my plan to steal his identification papers.

Without pausing to examine Delarge, I turned and began running away from the village down the Cholet road.

The plan, which I had earlier rejected as unworkable, was now my only hope. On reaching the Trissots' house, I called softly for their dog, Fitou. Fortunately, he recognized my voice and came running towards me, wagging his tail. When I was sure that Fitou wouldn't betray me, I entered the house through the unlocked kitchen door and collected all the food I could carry. In the larder I found an unopened bottle of brandy. I shoved it into my pocket and slipped out as quietly as I had come.

I retraced my steps of earlier that night and managed to find Jerôme's hiding place without too much difficulty. It was deserted. As I was wondering how I could possibly find him, he emerged from the trees to my right.

'Can't be too careful, comrade,' he said with a grin, lowering his gun. 'I had to be sure you were on your own. Tell me, what brings you back here already? I thought you were coming tomorrow night.'

I was too exhausted to think of an explanation. After handing over the stolen food (but not the brandy, which I kept hidden in my coat pocket), I lay down and fell into a deep sleep.

I awoke in the early afternoon. At first I was disorientated; then, as the focus of my memory sharpened, I was seized with horror. Passion had transformed me into a criminal and an outcast. Like a leaf in a cruel wind, I was being carried headlong I knew not where. Images flashed by in my mind: the cowardly Jerôme hunched over his fire, Delarge tumbling into the road, my mother in her powder blue dress . . .

I had made a terrible mistake. Although I had done no wrong — I had hit Delarge in self-defence, after all — by running away I had made myself appear guilty. My stupidity had left me with only one option. I had to close my mind to the past and concentrate, step by step, on carrying out my plan.

My first task, getting Jerôme drunk, was the easiest of all. As soon as he saw I was awake, he asked me whether I'd brought him a drink. I smiled and handed over the stolen brandy. Calling me the 'finest comrade since Marx himself', Jerôme pulled out the cork and took a heavy swig. An hour and a half later he had finished the entire bottle and lay snoring in a drunken stupor.

When I was sure he was insensible, I began searching for his identity papers. I found them, wrapped in an oilskin

47

cloth to protect them from the damp, hidden inside the lining of his coat. It took only seconds to swap them for my own. Minutes later, leaving Pierre Clouet asleep beside his camp fire, I was on the move again.

Jerôme, the second son of Jean-Luc and Anne Villequin from the city of Orléans, born 5 July 1896, was going to re-join the army.

Twelve

The Army

It is often said that Fortune favours the brave. This, as any soldier will tell you, is nonsense. Fortune is blind. She distributes her favours at random, on heroes and cowards alike. It was pure chance, therefore, that on 10 April 1915 she happened to be smiling on me.

I had made my way to La Roche-sur-Yon, the administrative capital of the Vendée, and was standing at the counter of the local recruiting office. An elderly sergeant was staring suspiciously at my papers.

'I admire your pluck, lad,' he said dryly, 'but if you're Jerôme Villequin from Orléans, then I'm Joan of Arc. Your accent's wrong for a start. And where did you get these papers from, anyway? Steal 'em, did you?'

At that moment someone came into the room behind me. I turned and found myself staring straight at Captain Brissot, the officer who had set up the St Frévisse Recruitment Committee.

To my astonishment, Brissot did not challenge me. He stared at me for a few seconds then, quite deliberately, winked at me and tapped the side of his nose with his finger.

The sergeant, who had been glancing over my papers again, looked up and said, 'Excuse me, Captain, but we've got a problem here. This young man says he's Jerôme Villequin from Orléans . . .'

'That's right, Sergeant!' interrupted Brissot. 'His family's been in the Vendée for a while now. I signed up his father. Jerôme's OK, Sergeant. Sign him up straight away. We need all the men we can get, don't we?'

He turned and left the room.

The sergeant handed my false papers back to me and said with a knowing look, 'Friends in high places, eh? Well, all I can say, *Monsieur Villequin*, is that you're a lucky young man. Very lucky indeed.'

If someone had told me in March that I would be in the army in a month's time, I would have agreed with the sergeant. I was indeed lucky to have achieved my ambition. But the way I had done it – sneaking through as a criminal with false papers – meant I felt little joy.

My conscience plagued me. I had discovered a deserter and not turned him in, killed a man and abandoned my widowed mother at a time when she needed me most.

Over the next few months I sometimes imagined what was happening in St Frévisse. With Delarge gone, I wondered who was running the bakery. I pictured Aurelie telling her friends that she had always thought I was a bit odd. I wondered if Jerôme had been caught and, if so, what he had said about me. And I saw my mother, tight-lipped in her misery, wondering what had happened on the night I disappeared. I prayed that she knew I was thinking of her.

I desperately wanted to write to my mother, to set the record straight. But that was impossible – all letters were read by an officer, so everything I wrote would become public knowledge.

Through my painful heart-searching I was kept going by a dream. In battle my brave deeds would avenge the deaths of Bruno, Louis and Papa. I would be a hero, awarded medals for my gallantry. Then, and only then, I would explain about Delarge and Jerôme, and my petty deception would be forgiven. Cheering crowds would gather to welcome me back to St Frévisse . . . Aurelie would apologize for thinking badly of me . . . Mama would weep with joy . . .

My dream began to cloud over long before I saw any fighting. Our training camp was perched on the side of a windy hill somewhere south of Paris. The food was dull, the routine tedious, our officers bullying or bored. To my annoyance, they nicknamed me 'Sonny', because of my youthful looks and enthusiasm.

Even the uniform was uninspiring. The recruits of 1914 had worn magnificent red jackets and bright blue trousers. We were issued with grey-blue uniforms made of some cheap, heavy woollen material that was too hot in the summer and soaked up the rain like a sponge in the winter.

For three long months we were instructed how to march, fire our rifles, stab sacks of straw with our bayonets – and dig trenches. Once, while we were hacking out a trench across a stony field in the blazing sun, I asked our corporal how digging holes would help us get to Berlin.

He stared at me with pity and contempt. 'What's that over there, Sonny?' he sneered, pointing to a giant steel insect in the corner of the field.

I prided myself on my military knowledge. 'It's an eight-millimetre Hotchkiss machine gun, sir.'

'Very good, Villequin! And how many rounds does it fire in a minute?'

'Six hundred, sir!'

'Excellent! And how far do you think you'd get running towards a gun like that when it was firing at you?'

'Er, about ten metres, sir?' I suggested.

'With luck, Villequin. So if you can't dig a trench, we'll have to dig one for you. Two metres deep. It's called a grave, Sonny. Now, get back to work before I have you doubling round the field with that gun on your pathetic shoulders!'

Thirteen

Fear

Most of the recruits who trained with me were sent to the reserve. Only a handful, mostly young men who had distinguished themselves in some way, were allocated to front-line divisions. I was immensely proud to be included in their number. We were to become part of the Second Army, replacing troops that had been killed or wounded in battle.

When I joined the famous 'Iron' (20th Infantry) Corps in the middle of July it was camped south of Rheims, well behind the front lines. My new colleagues were veterans of several battles. They weren't at all as I imagined they would be. Although still in their twenties, their gaunt faces made them look much older. They didn't talk about the war, either. When I asked them what going into battle was like, they shrugged and told me I'd find out soon enough. The conspiracy of silence confused me. It reminded me of how Papa had written

54

about wild flowers rather than killing Germans.

Something didn't add up. The newspapers and military command remained optimistic. Things had not gone too well, they admitted, and regrettably there had been heavy casualties. But now the French armies had been reorganized and re-equipped. Our British allies had increased the size of their forces, too. Moreover, the Germans had to fight on two fronts: the Russians in the east and ourselves in the west. The tide of the war was turning. Soon there would be a new, unstoppable offensive that would bring the war to a victorious conclusion by the end of 1915.

But the men of the 20th Infantry were more cynical, none more so than our section commander, Antoine Cousseau. When I mentioned that I had heard the war would be over by Christmas, he just snorted.

'You think the report's wrong, sir?' I asked.

'No, it's not wrong, Sonny,' he replied. 'The war *will* be over by Christmas – Christmas *1925*.'

I thought it rather a bad joke.

In August it was our turn to go to the front line. At last, I thought, a chance to revive my fading dream of glory! We moved into position at night, stumbling down the zigzagging communication trench and taking up positions in the dark.

At dawn, Cousseau made his inspection. 'Happier now, Sonny?' he asked.

'Yes, sir!' I replied eagerly. 'But it's a bit strange not being able to see the enemy.'

'Just as well, soldier. It means he can't see you.'

He began to move on, then turned back and took off my helmet. 'I think it's time you learned something, Sonny,' he said wearily. 'Before you get yourself killed. Watch!'

He placed my helmet over the muzzle of my rifle and lifted it above the top of the trench. Seconds later a machine gun started firing from the German lines. There was a metallic clanging above our heads.

Cousseau lowered my rifle. I stared in disbelief at the four gaping holes in my helmet. The bullets had passed right through.

'Got the message, Sonny?' grinned Cousseau. I nodded, too shaken to speak. 'Good, then I suggest you go and get yourself a new helmet.'

When he had gone, I leaned against the side of the trench. I was shivering and sweating at the same time. It wasn't a fever, but something I had never before experienced.

Instinctive, overwhelming fear.

We remained at the front for four weeks, unwashed, tired and bored, but unharmed. The nearest we came to action was when the enemy lobbed an occasional shell across no-man's-land or splattered the parapet of our trench with machine-gun fire.

As we retired towards Rheims after our spell at the front, we passed row upon row of massive guns. The road was clogged with men, lorries and horses moving in the opposite direction. It was impossible to ignore the rumours: the autumn offensive, the assault that would signal the beginning of the end for Germany, was about to begin.

The 20th Infantry was ordered to lead the second wave of attacks, taking over after the capture of the enemy's advanced positions. We never left our trench. In our sector the assault troops didn't even reach the enemy line, let alone take it.

The sounds, smells and sights that I experienced that day will remain with me for ever. It was my first taste of war, stripped of its false glory and romance, in all its naked, heart-breaking terribleness.

Through the narrow portholes of my gas mask I watched clouds of yellow poison foul the morning air. A hellish chorus of whines and crashes blotted out the band that played as the men went over the top. The earth heaved. Wounded men squealed like pigs. Guns spat. Bodies jerked and fell in heaps. Everywhere was pain, blood and inevitable death.

Now I understood it all: my father's sudden interest in flowers, Jerôme's desertion, the sergeant's scorn, the veterans' silence and, yes, even Delarge's cowardice.

I pitied them all because I pitied myself.

Fourteen

A Killing

The attacks continued until the end of October. On two occasions the 20th Infantry was sent over the top first, straight into the murderous hail of bullets and shells. Somehow I survived.

Once I even reached the enemy front line and saw my first German. We met in the trench, head on – I would have said face to face, but we were both wearing gas masks and so had no faces. We were just grotesque shapes, like caricature beasts at a macabre fancy-dress ball.

For an instant, shocked at finding the enemy semi-human after all, we just stared at each other. I moved first. My bayonet cut into the side of his neck. Blood pumped from the wound, splattering against the glass eye-pieces of my gas mask. I wiped it away in time to see him slipping slowly to the trench floor. He didn't scream or cry out, but died with muffled gurgling.

I was glad I had not seen his face.

An hour later the retreat sounded. We abandoned the trench we had captured and hurried back to our own lines.

Five weeks of fighting destroyed my dream of glory for ever. It was Cousseau who made me see how I had changed. Late one wet afternoon, a week after the offensive had been called off, he approached me as I was cleaning my rifle.

'When you've finished your weapon, Sonny,' he said in his usual terse manner, 'do something about your uniform! It's a disgrace to the 20th Infantry!'

I glanced down at the dark stain left by the blood of the man I had killed. 'I've tried to wash it out, sir. But it seems permanent.'

'Permanent, Sonny? Nothing's permanent around here. You should understand that by now.'

'Yes, I do understand it, sir,' I replied. Surprised and strangely disturbed by his pessimistic tone, I spoke without really thinking what I was saying.

Cousseau looked at me for a moment. His grey eyes remained as expressionless as ever, but when he spoke his voice was softer, almost kindly, 'Then you know what it means, don't you, soldier?'

'Yes, sir. I think so, sir,' I stammered. Cousseau had called me 'soldier' for the first time. That and his friendly manner upset me more than his shouting and sarcasm had ever done. I swallowed and wiped my eyes with my sleeve.

Cousseau ignored my distress. 'Tell me the truth, soldier – how old are you?' he asked.

'Eighteen, sir. You have to be eighteen to enlist . . .'

'Of course. Eighteen.' Bending his head towards me so we wouldn't be overheard, he continued, 'Listen, soldier. I wasn't born yesterday. I've noticed you don't write letters. Not one since you joined us. There are two reasons why soldiers don't write: either they're having a breakdown or they've got something to hide. You're not breaking up, are you, soldier?'

'No, sir!'

'Then there's something you don't want known. Right?'

'I, er, don't know, sir,' I muttered.

What I took for a smile passed across Cousseau's face. 'Of course you know, soldier! Listen. Someone, somewhere wants to hear from you. And you ought to get in touch with them. You don't want to leave it too late, do you?'

He paused for the remark to sink in, then continued, 'I'll make a bargain with you, young Villequin. If you write home and promise not to mention anything that might be useful to the enemy, I'll see your letter's not read by anyone before it's sent. Not even the name on the envelope. Agreed?'

I was stunned. Cousseau knew me better than I knew myself. I had to trust him. 'Agreed, sir.' I said nervously. 'And thank you, sir.'

Cousseau stood upright and said in his usual, military manner, 'Right, soldier! Now we've sorted that out, perhaps you'll be so good as to get yourself looking worthy of the 20th Infantry!'

That evening I began the first letter I had ever written to Mama. After several false starts, I decided to tell her everything. I told her what I knew about Delarge and how I suspected he was a fraud. I told her about Jerôme Villequin, my plan and the truth about my fight with Delarge. And I told her how I had joined up with false papers and was now at the front with one of the most respected units in the army.

But I did not tell her – I could not tell her – what I had seen and heard in the last few months. About the horror, the suffering, the brutality, the endless killing I said nothing. It was not a matter of giving away military secrets. Even if I had been allowed to write about life at the front, I could not have done so. Such awfulness was beyond description.

I have rarely felt such relief as when I handed over my unsealed letter to Cousseau. It was as if I had made a confession to a priest. My conscience was clear. My sins, I was sure, would be understood and forgiven. I no longer had to prove myself with acts of heroism.

All I had to do now was survive.

Fifteen

Verdun

The winter months were dreary. The last thing I had expected the war to be was boring, but the long days spent in sodden trenches were extremely tedious. We passed more time trying to keep warm and dry than worrying about the enemy. The only things we shot at were the rats that had descended on the battlefield in their thousands to feed off the corpses left rotting in no-man's-land.

My only hope at the start of each day was that I might hear from Mama. But no letter came. As the weeks went by, I began to fear that my confession had not reached her and that I would die without her ever knowing the truth.

There had been one significant development, however. At least, it was significant for me. About a week after I had written to Mama a new officer joined the 20th Infantry. I say 'new', but in fact Captain Frissot had been in the army since long before the outbreak of war. He was one of the old school: fierce, rigid and totally unsympathetic. His narrow face and darting eyes reminded me of Delarge. I was instinctively wary of him.

Shortly after Frissot's arrival I was given ample grounds for my suspicion. We were in the third line of our defences, resting after our tour of duty in the front line, when Frissot made what he called a 'Getting-to-know-my-men' visit. We stood to attention with our backs to the sodden trench wall most of the morning as he passed slowly round. He made a point of talking to each man in turn.

When he reached me, Frissot looked me casually up and down before asking, 'Name, soldier?'

'Private Jerôme Villequin, sir!'

He looked startled. 'Did you say "Villequin", soldier?'

'I did, sir!'

'And where are you from?'

'Orléans, sir!'

Frissot turned to Cousseau, who was accompanying him. 'It's strange, Corporal,' he said, 'but I used to have another Jerôme Villequin from Orléans under my command. A cowardly, left-wing wimp. He deserted.'

Frissot turned back to me. 'You're not cowardly, are you, soldier?'

'No, sir!' I replied as vehemently as I could.

'Nor left-wing, nor a deserter by any chance?' Frissot demanded.

'No way, sir!'

Frissot nodded uncertainly. 'Maybe. Remind me to check this man's records, Corporal Cousseau.'

As he passed by on his way to the next man, Cousseau drew in his breath and gave me a look as if to say, 'Watch your step, soldier! This officer is trouble!'

I don't know whether Frissot had a look at my records that evening. I doubt it, for he was usually drunk by nightfall and incapable of handling paperwork. I doubted, too, whether Cousseau reminded him. The corporal knew a good soldier when he saw one and didn't want to lose me.

Several weeks later, on 21 February 1916, a thunderous artillery barrage opened up far away to our right. Cousseau told us the sound came from the direction of Verdun. He added, with a rare flash of humour, 'I don't fancy the Boche's chances in that sector: it's got more forts and castles per square metre than Le Touquet Beach in August!'

By midday, however, the noise had not abated. Even Cousseau was looking concerned. At 1 am we were told to prepare for action. Half an hour later a second order came round. The 20th Infantry was to retire at once and prepare for a route march. We were urgently needed to reinforce the front fifty kilometres to the east.

'To the east, Corporal?' asked one of the men as we lined up in the road behind our lines. 'Where's that, then?'

'I told you before,' said Cousseau, clearly anxious. 'Listen!' The angry rumble of the barrage was still clearly audible behind us.

'Ah!' grinned the man. 'You mean we're going to Le Touquet!'

'Shut up!' snapped Cousseau. 'If Verdun needs us, soldier, it means trouble. We're not going on a holiday, I promise you!'

We marched for almost two days, stopping only briefly to eat and snatch a few hours sleep. Late in the afternoon of the first day the incessant noise of heavy artillery was replaced by the intermittent firing of smaller guns. We knew at once what it meant – the attack had begun.

On the second day clouds of smoke blackened the horizon. Shells exploded on either side of the road, showering us with mud. Once or twice we were forced to make a detour into the fields to avoid a gaping crater. Casualties, some walking, some on stretchers, some in ambulances, streamed past us in the opposite direction. The orderlies accompanying them stared at us with blank, pitying faces.

On the morning of 23 February we reached Verdun, a broken ruin of a town with scarcely a building intact. Still we marched on, over the River Meuse and into the broken, pock-marked landscape beyond. Finally, in the smouldering skeleton that had once been the village of Bras, we halted.

Not even the Iron Corps could go into battle without a rest. We needed all the strength we could muster for the ominous battle ahead.

Sixteen

Suicide Mission

I have been told that the aim of the German attack on Verdun was to 'bleed the French army white'. If this was so, they chose the right place for the attempt.

The front line around the ancient town bulged like a blister into enemy-occupied territory. Those of us in the forward positions were assailed and bombarded from the north, east and west. Our army was like a boxer in a ring with three opponents: we never knew where the next blow would come from.

What were we doing there? When General Pétain took command, his first order to us was chillingly simple: 'Hold fast!' We recognized at once that it was not Verdun we were defending but the honour of France.

So began a battle of wills, a trial of national strength and endurance. The Germans believed we would lose either the town or our army. We were determined, because we were the Iron Corps, to lose neither.

At dawn on 24 February, after a night of shelling, we were ordered to dig in along a small country road that led to the village of Louvemont. It was not a good defensive position. We were overlooked by a low hill whose wooded slopes gave the enemy excellent protection. At least fifty men were hit by sniper fire as we hacked and scraped at the flinty soil.

By the evening we had linked a series of shell craters with a row of trenches. During the night engineers constructed a barbed-wire fence about ten metres in front of our line. Now, we reckoned, we could hold out against whatever the enemy threw at us. We did not have long to wait before our theory was tested.

The bombardment began at mid-morning and lasted for about an hour. It was intended to soften us up, but was so inaccurate that I don't think our part of the line suffered any casualties at all.

The shelling ceased abruptly at midday. Immediately, the wood in front of us came alive. Hundreds, perhaps thousands, of enemy soldiers emerged from the trees and began advancing towards us like an army of ants.

'Hold your fire!' called Cousseau. 'Wait for the command!'

Peering over the top of our trench, rifles at the ready, we watched the enemy draw steadily closer. The shouts of their officers were clearly audible in the still winter air. I was vaguely aware of machine-gun fire away to my left.

When the Germans were no more than four hundred metres distant, a bugle sounded.

'Take aim!' cried Cousseau. 'Make every shot count – and – *fire!*'

Rifles cracked and machine guns hammered all along the line. Within seconds the enemy's first line had disappeared, as if wiped away by some magic hand. The second took their place, stepping over the bodies of fallen comrades and hurrying on towards us.

The orderly advance had been broken. Some men were sprinting towards us, zigzagging to avoid the bullets. Others knelt down to return our fire. A few were already hurrying back towards the safety of the trees.

Directly before me an officer was waving his arms and yelling frantically at his men. I calmly fixed him in my sights and squeezed the trigger.

It was child's play, like target shooting at a fairground. When the bullet hit him he froze for an instant, as if surprised at what had happened. Then, very slowly, his knees gave way and he folded like a puppet into the grass.

The killing was so easy.

Our little victory was important to us. But its only effect on the battle as a whole was to prove that the German advance could be halted. We were punished for our success, too. The next day we were subjected to a four-hour bombardment of vicious accuracy.

A fortnight later we were forced to abandon our position and fall back towards Charny.

Our new line, on a ridge above the River Meuse, was better chosen. We had a clear view of the land in front of us and there were no woods for the enemy to shelter in. The only drawback was a ruined farm high to our right. The enemy had captured it earlier in the battle and set up a nest of machine guns there. Any movement in our trenches drew a hail of murderous fire.

After shelling had failed to dislodge the machine gunners, Captain Frissot decided the farm could be taken by a small patrol of infantry operating under the cover of darkness. It was a crazy idea. The ground between us and the buildings was wide open. If any sound was made, flares would go up and the patrol would be sitting ducks.

Cousseau described the plan as a 'suicide mission' and strongly objected to it. Frissot overruled him. It was his scheme and he was proud of it. He even insisted on selecting the patrol himself.

My name was at the top of his list.

Seventeen

The Angel

Frissot's plan was as ill-prepared as it was idiotic. On the evening of the attack he summoned us to his command bunker to give us our orders. Our mission was simple: make our way to the farm and 'take out' the machine gunners. We were not told how or what to do if something went wrong.

'Just do it,' Frissot said firmly. 'If you don't think of failing, you won't. War's all in the mind, you know.'

When one of the patrol pointed out that there was a full moon, Frissot laughed and said sarcastically, 'Well done, soldier! Exactly when the enemy will be least expecting you.'

He might have said the same for the weather, too. The night was cold and cloudless.

We were due to set out at 2 am. With a final touch of stupidity, Frissot had arranged for the artillery to fire a few shells at 1.45. 'A diversion,' he explained. 'An old tactic, I know, but it usually works.'

It wasn't worth mentioning to him that even if the occupants of the farm were dozing beforehand, the shelling would make sure they were wide-awake by the time we appeared on the scene.

As we filed out of the dugout, Frissot stopped me. 'Here's your chance, Villequin,' he said, standing so close that I could smell the liquor on his breath.

I looked at him blankly.

'Don't play that game with me, soldier!' he said angrily. 'Deserter or not, if you succeed tonight, I'll forget what I know. Wipe the slate clean, eh?'

I saluted and went out into the night. I knew he didn't mean it. He wasn't going to wipe any slate clean. He wouldn't have to. This patrol was just a way of getting rid of a problem that had been worrying him since he had joined us. Captain Frissot knew as well as I did what was going to happen. The entire patrol would be wiped out long before we reached the machine guns.

We got further than I expected. The farm stood about five hundred metres from our lines. We had covered about half this distance, crawling on our bellies over the frozen ground, when the first flare arched into the night sky and cast its brilliant white glare over the battlefield. I flattened myself into the ground and waited for the inevitable onslaught.

To my surprise, not a single shot was fired. After waiting ten minutes, we began to move slowly forward again. A second flare was fired. Again we froze and again nothing happened.

I was beginning to think luck was with us when there was a loud metallic clang somewhere to my left. One of our men had accidentally hit his rifle against a piece of debris – an empty shell case, perhaps – left lying on the battlefield.

The sound acted like an alarm bell. Four or five flares immediately soared into the air above our heads. A machine gun opened up. Then another. A mortar bomb exploded behind us. Within a minute we were engulfed by a roaring avalanche of bullets, bombs and shells.

I pressed my face into the earth and waited for the end. I prayed it would be swift. No soldier wanted to be left to die a slow and painful death, alone and untended in no-man's-land.

A shell landed just in front of me. The earth rose up, flinging me backwards. No sooner had I hit the ground, than I was hurled into the air by another explosion.

There was no more noise. I watched the stars slipping slowly by as I spun like a sycamore seed over and over and over . . .

I briefly recovered consciousness to see Cousseau bending

over me. He felt my pulse then lifted me carefully on to his shoulder and started to run.

Much later, I learned that he got within ten metres of our trenches before a burst of machine-gun fire ripped through his spine. He died instantly. Two other men risked their lives to drag me to safety.

They said I was dying, the men who carried me on a stretcher to the first-aid station. The pain in my legs was so great I hoped they were right. I closed my eyes and drifted away from them into a tortured world of my own.

Long hours of jolting. Low moaning. Bright lights. Voices, muffled and resigned. And always the same, screaming pain.

Was this heaven, this darkened room that smelt of death and disinfectant? A lady dressed all in white floated before me. She approached and stroked my brow. Oh! This was heaven indeed! I was being ministered to by an angel.

I had seen her blurred face before, this graceful creature, but I could not remember where. Was it in the stained glass behind the altar of the church at St Frévisse? No, this was a living angel.

I rolled my head towards her. She smiled a sweet, familiar smile. Just like my mother's.

Even in death, it seemed, she had not deserted me.

Eighteen

A Survivor

She *was* my mother, that angel who nursed me back to life.

Both my legs were broken in several places. I had gashes on my face and body that took weeks to heal and left me permanently scarred. My left ear drum had been blown in, leaving me partially deaf. Worse still, perhaps, I was profoundly shocked. For many months the slightest sudden noise – even a door slamming – sent me diving for cover. Even now, I break out in a cold sweat at the sound of a farmer shooting pigeons.

It was some time before I could tell Mama what had happened to me. In the meantime, bit by bit, she related her story.

To my intense relief she assured me that her relationship with Delarge had never been more than a mild flirtation. She had been flattered by his attentions, she admitted, but had never given him reason to hope that one day she would be his. Indeed, on the night of our fight on the

Cholet road she had told him to leave her alone. He had reacted like a child, first pleading with her and then threatening. Had I been there to take charge, she would have sacked him from the bakery immediately.

I had not killed Delarge. He had, I imagine, merely knocked himself out when he fell. The next day he explained his injuries by saying he had tripped over in the dark on the way to work. Of the deserter, Jerôme Villequin, Mama had heard not a word. We assumed that he had managed to find a ship to take him to America.

My disappearance had remained a complete mystery for many months. Mama, who knew I had wanted to join the army, had her suspicions. But as Captain Brissot denied having seen me, she was none the wiser. As the weeks passed, she began to fear that she would never see me again.

The arrival of my letter in early December 1915 changed everything. Not wishing to alert Delarge, Mama kept its contents to herself. She had taken a greater interest in the family business since I had gone. Now, pretending she needed information for the tax office, she questioned Delarge about his past. When his answers were unconvincing, she asked the authorities to investigate. He was arrested at the end of the month and driven away in handcuffs. Mama heard later that he had been shot for desertion.

Late one afternoon, enjoying the summer sunshine on the hospital veranda, I finally asked the question that had been nagging me for ages.

'Tell me, Mama, why didn't you write to me?'

'Write to you, Pierre? Why, I wrote to you almost every day! Didn't you receive my letters?'

I replied that I hadn't received a single line. To this day I still don't know the reason. Not wishing to betray me, Mama had addressed her letters to Jerôme Villequin of the 20th Infantry. Yet not one had been delivered. I can only assume that they were intercepted by Captain Frissot and destroyed.

At the end of 1915, not having heard from me, Mama had assumed the worst. The war had taken both her husband and her son and she had little to live for. She had volunteered as an auxiliary nurse. It was the only practical way she knew to help lessen the terrible suffering of war.

After a brief training, she was hurried to the Verdun sector. There, by what she believed was a miracle, she had found me. The doctors gave me little chance of survival and more than once she was told off for spending too much time on a patient almost certain to die.

But Mama never believed the doctors. Now she was with me, she felt certain I would pull through. The moment I recognized her was the happiest of her life.

'Do you know that when you first came round you called me an angel?' she smiled.

'We all make mistakes,' I teased.

Her face grew serious. 'Yes, Pierre, we all do. And we live to regret them, too.'

We sat in silence for a few minutes, thinking over what she had said. 'And now?' she asked eventually.

I shrugged. 'First I must learn to walk again. After that, well, I don't suppose the army will want me back.'

'No, Pierre,' said Mama firmly, 'it certainly won't.'

'Why are you so certain?'

'To begin with, you're not old enough.'

'But they don't know . . . Mama, you haven't told them, have you? '

'Of course I have, Pierre!' she said softly. 'And there's nothing to worry about. I received the letter this morning. Pierre Clouet has been honourably discharged and all mention of Jerôme Villequin of the 20th Infantry has been wiped from the records.'

'You mean I don't exist?'

'No, Pierre. It's only your past that has gone. You're one of the lucky ones. A survivor. Unlike countless others, you still have a future.'

Historical Notes

The Battle of Verdun continued until December 1916. By this time about 10 million shells had been fired and nine villages wiped from the map. The French had lost about 378,000 men and the Germans 337,000.

The ruined town of Verdun remained in French hands. Moreover, a series of bloody counter-attacks at the end of the year had recaptured much of the ground lost to the Germans in February 1916. The French army had not quite been 'bled white' and was still able to defend its sectors of the Western Front. Technically speaking, therefore, the Battle of Verdun was a French victory.

To speak of 'victory', however, is pointless. The morale of both the French and German armies had been irreparably damaged. The Germans launched no large-scale offensives during 1917. A French offensive in the Champagne region in April–May 1917 provoked serious mutinies among the troops.

After Verdun the war dragged on for another twenty-two months. It was a naval blockade, not defeat on the battlefield, that finally caused Germany to surrender. When the guns fell silent on 11 November 1918, the German army was still in possession of territory it had captured in its 1914 offensive.

The humiliating peace terms imposed on Germany in 1919 did not last and twenty years later France and Germany were at war again. The ghastly bloodshed had settled nothing: that was the ultimate tragedy of Verdun – indeed, of the whole war.

Further Information

If you would like to know more about Verdun and World War I, these are among the many books on the subject:

Martin, Gilbert, *First World War* (HarperCollins, 1997)

Grant, Reg, *Armistice, 1918* (Hodder Wayland, 2000)

Hansen, Ole Steen, *The War in the Trenches* (Hodder Wayland, 2000)

Keegan, John, *The First World War* (Hutchinson, 1998)

Mason, David, *Verdun* (Windrush, 2000)

Ross, Stewart, *Leaders of World War I* (Hodder Wayland, 2002)

Ross, Stewart, *Causes of World War I* (Hodder Wayland, 2002)

Ross, Stewart, *Technology of World War I* (Hodder Wayland, 2002)

Of the many websites with useful information on World War I, these two make reliable starting points:

www.bbc.co.uk/history/war/wwone/index.shtml
www.iwm.org.uk/online/index.htm

Glossary

Anisette A popular aniseed-tasting spirit.

Artillery Heavy guns.

Auxiliary nurse An assistant nurse.

Boche A slang term for a German, used during the war.

Bunker An underground shelter.

Communication trench A trench running between first, second and third line trenches, usually in a zigzag pattern.

Conscription Compulsory service in the armed forces.

Department A French administrative division, like a British county.

Deserter Someone who leaves the armed forces without permission.

Dugout A temporary shelter dug into the ground and covered with a roof of wood and earth.

Flare An inflammable substance fired into the air at night to illuminate the terrain (or send a signal).

Fraternity Friendship or citizenship.

Front The nearest point of an army to the enemy.

Imperialist Someone who is enthusiastic about their country's empire.

Left-wing Inclined towards communism or socialism.

Le Touquet A fashionable seaside resort in north-west France.

Mortar A device that fires bombs over a short range.

Naval blockade Using the navy to cut off a country's supplies of food and raw materials.

No-man's-land Unoccupied land between two armies' front lines.

Oilskin A waterproof cloth.

Reparations Payment in compensation for a wrong done.

Shell An exploding missile fired by the artillery.

Telegraph An electronic device for sending coded messages down a wire.

Veteran Someone who has fought in a past war.

Western Front The battle front in Western Europe, 1914–18. It comprised two lines of opposing trenches and other defences that stretched from the Channel to the Swiss border.

ONLY A MATTER OF TIME

Stewart Ross

'We are the future, Drita. You and me, Albanian and Serb, good friends. It's the way it must be in Kosovo.'

When I think now how innocent we were, it makes me cry.

It's early in 1999 when Drita, an Albanian, and Zoran, a Serb, become friends. They're just like any other teenagers. But this is Kosovo, and Serb–Albanian tension is rising. Drita and Zoran find that their families are now enemies and the couple are forced to meet in secret. The events that follow are enough to blow apart even the strongest of friendships and Drita and Zoran are about to begin a fight for their lives. Will their friendship survive?

THE STAR HOUSES

Stewart Ross

Snipping away the stitching that held on my yellow star, my mother said defiantly, 'Right! That's simple. From now on we won't wear these silly badges. None of us!' When she had finished, she exclaimed, 'There! Now you're just an ordinary Hungarian like everyone else.' If only it had been that simple.

Bandi Guttmann is a fourteen-year-old Hungarian Jew, living in Budapest in 1944. German forces have occupied the city and life for Bandi and his family is about to become unbearable. Set apart from the rest of the Hungarian community, and denied basic human rights, the family's only weapon is their determination to survive. But in the face of mindless hatred, will the Guttmanns' strength, love and courage be enough to hold them together?

The Star Houses is based on the memoirs of Andor Guttmann.